P9-DDU-475

First published in the United States of America in 2015 by Chronicle Books LLC.
Originally published in France in 2013 under the title *Ma famille sauvage* by hélium/Actes Sud, 18 rue Séguier, 75006 Paris.

Library of Congress Cataloging-in-Publication Data available.
ISBN 978-1-4521-4423-8

Manufactured in China.

Typeset in Brandon Printed and Brandon Text.

10 9 8 7 6 5 4 3 2 1

Chronicle Books LLC
680 Second Street
San Francisco, California 94107

Chronicle Books—we see things differently.
Become part of our community at www.chroniclekids.com.

MY WILD FAMILY

Laurent Moreau

chronicle books · san francisco

I HAVE A VERY
SPECIAL FAMILY.

• MY OLDER BROTHER •

He's strong and respected. (Just don't upset him.)

• MY LITTLE BROTHER •

Flighty and a dreamer, his head is often in the clouds.

He's also an excellent singer.

2 =
123
456

• MY MOTHER •

Tall and beautiful, everyone notices her.

She is also shy and prefers not to stand out.

• MY FATHER •

Very hairy, he can be fierce sometimes.

But when he's at the beach, he really relaxes.

• MY GRANDMOTHER •

Sweet and generous, she likes to stay home.

She has very good hearing, especially for her TV.

• MY GRANDFATHER •

He may be tired and slow,

but he always gets up so ladies may have a seat.

267

• MY AUNT •

Always perfectly primped, she never leaves the house without looking her best.

• MY UNCLE •

He devours anything and everything. It's impressive how much he can eat!

• MY COUSINS •

They're fast and flexible,

always quick to monkey around.

• MY BEST FRIEND •

She makes the best scary faces.

But don't be fooled! She's actually quite funny.

MY OTHER BEST FRIEND

He's as fast as the wind—just *try* to outrun him! He breaks all records.

My family is truly special. And me . . .

well, you might say I'm unique, too.

AND YOU?

WHAT MAKES YOU SPECIAL?